Tumble Tails

Tilley Tumble:
The Tumbling Bunny

For Simon and Charlie, with love x

For Emily, my very own tumbling bunny!

First published 2018. This edition published 2019.

Text and illustrations by Beth Thompson © 2018.

Published by Aireborough Press.

ISBN: 978-1-9164680-0-9

Second edition

Aireborough Press: hello@aireboroughpress.com

Tumble Tails

Tilley Tumble:
The Tumbling Bunny

Written and Illustrated by Beth Thompson

Tilley Tumble was the busiest, bounciest and bendiest little bunny in Barley Burrow.

Tilley loved to bounce through the meadow chasing butterflies, but more than anything in the world, she loved gymnastics.

She dreamed that one day she might become a famous gymnastics superstar.

Daddy Tumble joked that Tilley could walk on her hands before she could walk on her feet! She practiced gymnastics, every day and every night. Sometimes in the garden...

but mostly on Mommy and Daddy's bed!

Tilley Tumble just could not keep still!

She leapt through Barley Burrow forest, and she rolled
through the fallen leaves.

She climbed to the top of the tallest trees, and she swung
from the highest branches.

Poor Mommy Tumble did not know what to do.

Whenever Tilley practiced gymnastics, she made such a mess!

She stepped on the cat's tail while perfecting her handstand.

She kicked over a vase of flowers while practicing her arabesque...

and she knocked over Mommy's favourite lamp while spinning on one leg!

One day at school, Tilley was given a leaflet about the opening of a new gym. Hoppa's Gymnastics Club was having an open day for all the bunnies of Barley Burrow.

Tilley popped the leaflet into her pocket....

and she cartwheeled all the way home -

without stopping!

On the morning of the open day, Tilley woke up early and
bounced out of bed. She hopped into her new leotard
and twirled around and around.

Tilley rushed downstairs and gobbled down her breakfast as fast as she could. "Daddy, is it time to go yet?" Tilley cried out for the hundredth time!

"Okay, my little Tumble, are you ready?" asked
Daddy Tumble.

"I'm ready!" Tilley squealed excitedly. Tilley picked up her
bag and hopped into the bunnymobile.

Tilley arrived at Hoppa's Gymnastics Club. Her nose
twitched and her tail trembled. She peered around
the door of the gym and gasped. "Wow!"

The gym was full of bunnies, big and small, jumping, leaping...

spinning and flipping through the air.

"Tilley? Tilley Tumble?" asked a voice behind her.

"I'm your coach, Miss Hoppa. Let's get started."

Tilley followed Miss Hoppa into the gym and joined a group
of bunnies for a warm up of fun games, with skipping and
bunny hops, bridges and spider walks.

"I can't do this - my ears are too long!" Tilley sobbed as she tried to swing from the gymnastics bar.

"Your ears are perfect," comforted Miss Hoppa. "Have another go."

Tilley took a deep breath. She pulled herself up onto the bar. Then she whizzed around and around the bar until she was so dizzy she could spin no more!

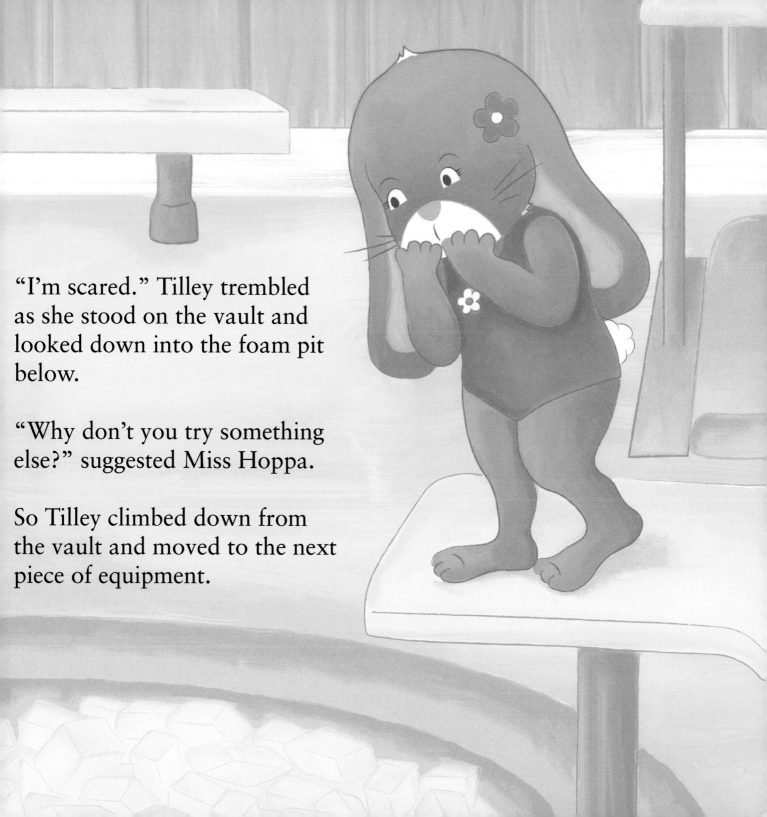

"I'm scared." Tilley trembled as she stood on the vault and looked down into the foam pit below.

"Why don't you try something else?" suggested Miss Hoppa.

So Tilley climbed down from the vault and moved to the next piece of equipment.

"I'm no good at this," cried Tilley as she tried to walk on the narrow balance beam. "My feet are too big!"

"Your feet are perfect," encouraged Miss Hoppa. "Try again."

Then, with a little help from Miss Hoppa, Tilley tiptoed the full length of beam.

"This is awesome!" squealed Tilley as she rolled, cartwheeled and leapt across the bouncy gymnastics floor.

"Great job, Tilley! You're a super little gymnast!" shouted Miss Hoppa.

Just before it was time to go home, Tilley attempted the vault one more time. Her nose twitched and her tail trembled.

She took a deep breath, then jumped off the vault and into the soft pit of foam. Miss Hoppa and the gym bunnies cheered, "Well done, Tilley!"

Tilley went to bed early that night. As she drifted off to sleep, she thought it had been the best day of her life so far. Then she dreamed the most wonderful dream about winning gold for Hoppa's at the World Bunny Gymnastics Championships.

The End

Meet the Author

Beth lives in Yorkshire, England, with her husband Simon, her two children Charlie and Emily, and their crazy Cockapoo, Monty. She likes to write and draw, sing and dance, and loves nothing more than a long walk in the countryside with her family.

Tilley Tumble is her first book. Tilley was inspired by Emily, who is a keen gymnast and spends most of her time upside down!

Look out for more adventures of Tilley Tumble and the bunnies of Barley Burrow coming very soon.

To be the first to read the next book in the series contact:
hello@aireboroughpress.com

Made in the USA
Monee, IL
16 December 2019